Spirit Bear: Fishing for Knowledge, Catching Dreams
Based on a True Story

Written by Cindy Blackstock

Illustrated by Amanda Strong

Edited by Jennifer King and Sarah Howden

First Nations Child & Family Caring Society of Canada
fncaringsociety.com | info@fncaringsociety.com | @Caringsociety

Art Direction and Illustration: Amanda Strong | spottedfawnproductions.com
Additional Illustration: Dora Cepic, Natty Boonmasiri, Rasheed Banda, Alex Mesa,
Bracken Hanuse Corlett, and Edwin Neel
Design and Layout: Leah Gryfe Designs | leahgryfedesigns.com

For help pronouncing the First Nations words in this book, please visit: **firstvoices.com**

In honour of the ancestors and Elders who are the keepers of traditional knowledge. To the children they share it with, and to Residential School Survivors who passed along as much good as they could to the generations that followed.

In special recognition of Shannen Koostachin, her family, Attawapiskat First Nation, and everyone who supports Shannen's Dream for "safe and comfy schools" for every First Nations student in Canada.

Visit **shannensdream.ca**

Hi, everyone! My name is Spirit Bear. I am a mem*bear* of the Carrier Sekani Tribal Council. But I spend most of my time on the lands of the Algonquin People in a city called Ottawa.

Ottawa is also where the Government of Canada lives. Governments make laws and provide the services that everyone needs—like clean water, education, and health care.

I have a pretty big job myself. I am a *Bearrister*, which means that when I see something wrong, I need to learn about it and help make things right. I take lots of trips by train (I love the train!) to visit and learn from people across the country.

I love to bake cookies, pick huckleberries, and go fishing!

Bear Author

BEARRISTER

Bear Actor

PAW hD
in Social Work
UVic

HONOURARY BEAR WITNESS

Bear Host of Teddy Bear Tea Parties and Bear Witness Day Parties

5

On my last trip, I learned about a big problem. The government in Ottawa gives less money to First Nations children than it does to other kids for things like schools, medical help, and even drinking water.

I know this is wrong—and I'm not the only one! I've met lots of children across Canada who want to make sure First Nations kids are treated fairly. Kids just like you!

I really want to make a difference, but I'm not sure what to do. So I decided to ask my mom, Mary the Bear.

"I'm so proud that you want to help," she said, while patting me on the back. "You should go talk to your Uncle Huckleberry. He's learned a lot over the years, especially from our bear ancestors. (Ancestors are all the ones who came before us.) Make sure to ask him about Shannen's Dream!"

7

LAKE
BEARBINE

8

Uncle Huckleberry is my mom's big brother. He's lived his whole life in the bush. We said "hi" with a big bear hug.

"Uncle Huckleberry, what was it like when you were a cub?"

"Things are a lot easier now, Spirit Bear!" said my uncle. "One day I will have to teach you our traditional way of fishing. We caught fish with our mouths back then. No fishing rods like today!"

"You must have gulped down lots of water!" I said, looking at the lake.

"Yup, but Lake Bearbine was a lot cleaner back then, and there were more fish and animals because the people took better care of it.

"In the old days, only the Carrier Sekani people lived here," Uncle Huckleberry continued. "They looked after the water and all the animals. But when the new people came, they started cutting down the trees, digging things like gold and silver out of the earth, and polluting the water."

"Can we make it better?" I asked.

"Yes, all children and cubs can help. You can recycle, support fish hatcheries, prevent forest fires, and make sure not to put bad stuff on the earth or in the water. You can also learn from First Nations peoples—they know how to look after the land and the animals."

I nodded and I listened closely so I would remember and be able to pass the knowledge down to the small cubs in my family.

"Where did the First Nations people go to school to learn all this stuff?"

"The world was their school, Spirit Bear," my uncle replied. "Grandpa Bearbine and Grandma Blueberry remember watching the Elders teach the children all kinds of important things, like how to care for the animals, themselves, and others with kindness and respect."

13

14

"Wow, children got to hang out with their grandparents *all the time*? That is *beary* COOL! What about recess?" I asked.

"Well, there wasn't recess back then like there is today," said Uncle Huckleberry. "Children learned from Elders by doing things together like cooking and storytelling. The Elders made learning fun, so children didn't really need a break to play."

"How did things change?" I wondered. "Why do kids today have to go to school in buildings and sit in rows?"

"Well..." Uncle Huckleberry began. Just then, a bear came wandering out of the woods behind us.

"Here is just the bear to answer your question," my uncle said. "It is our friend Lak'insxw from Gitxsan Territory!" *Lak'insxw* means "grizzly bear" in the Gitxsan language. Uncle Huckleberry gave a wave and Lak'insxw headed our way.

"Lak'insxw lives with the Gitxsan, who are neighbours to the Carrier Sekani. The Gitxsan people like salmon—and so does Lak'insxw."

"*Amma sah*, Huckleberry." (That means "good day" in Gitxsan.) "And you must be Spirit Bear. Good to meet you!" said Lak'insxw. "Huckleberry, can I pick lowbush blueberries in your territory? I will share my salmon with you!"

"Sure, but first, pull up a stump!" Uncle Huckleberry said. "I was just telling Spirit Bear how First Nations children went from being taught by Elders to going to schools. Since you travel so much, maybe you could tell him what you know." Lak'insxw nodded.

"The Elders taught First Nations children to live a good life from the knowledge handed down by their ancestors. Non-Indigenous children learned by going to schools and listening to teachers and reading books.

"All the children were happy learning in their different ways about one hundred and fifty years ago. That was when people in the government decided they should take First Nations children away from their families. The government did not want the children to be First Nations anymore. They wanted First Nations children to be like them, like non-Indigenous peoples."

I gulped. I know how much I love being a bear. I would not want someone trying to change me into something else. And I still need my family—especially my mom, Mary the Bear!

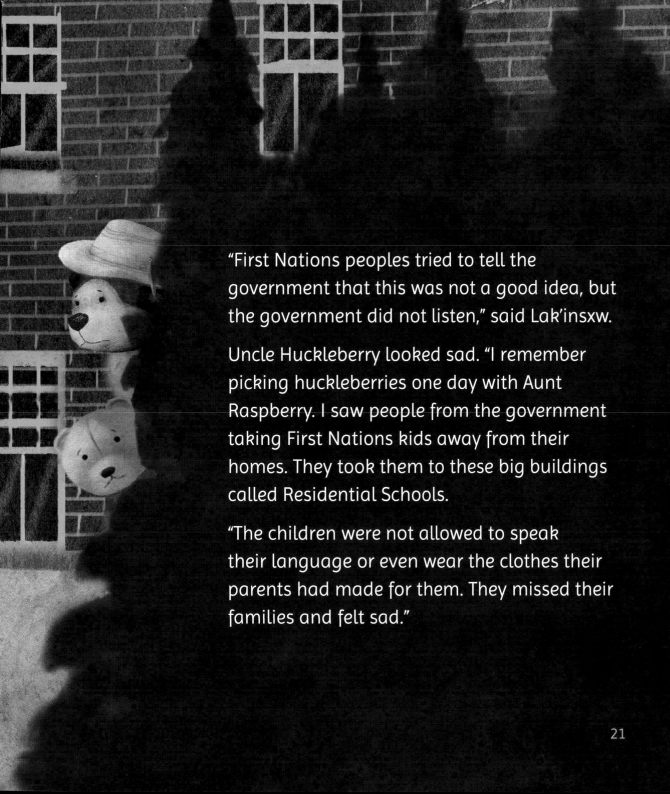

"First Nations peoples tried to tell the government that this was not a good idea, but the government did not listen," said Lak'insxw.

Uncle Huckleberry looked sad. "I remember picking huckleberries one day with Aunt Raspberry. I saw people from the government taking First Nations kids away from their homes. They took them to these big buildings called Residential Schools.

"The children were not allowed to speak their language or even wear the clothes their parents had made for them. They missed their families and felt sad."

"And their families were sad too," said Lak'insxw. "I travelled past First Nations communities where there were no children at all, because they were all in Residential Schools. The Elders had no children left to love and teach."

My heart felt heavy. "That is not right!" I said. "Why did the government do that to the First Nations children?"

"It happened to Métis and Inuit children, too," said Uncle Huckleberry, "because the government did not understand that First Nations, Métis, and Inuit children were special and important just the way they were."

23

"No one should do that to kids! They should close the Residential Schools down!" I said.

"Yes, Spirit Bear," Lak'insxw agreed. "The government finally did. The last one closed in 1996. But taking all those kids from their communities for so many years left a lot of sadness behind."

A tear rolled down my cheek.

Then I remembered what my mom told me. "What are First Nations schools like today? Mom said I should ask you about something called Shannen's Dream."

"Ah, yes," said Lak'insxw with a smile. "You need to go back to Ottawa and ask the children about Shannen Koostachin. Shannen is their hero."

26

"Good idea!" My uncle clapped his paws together. "Let's pack you a lunch of huckleberries, trout, and cookies for the train."

"How will I find the children when I get there?" I asked.

"Don't worry," said Lak'insxw. "The ancestors will guide you. Look up at the sky tonight, Spirit Bear."

I smiled. Another train trip—and cookies too!

"Hi! I'm Spirit Bear," I said to my new friends. "I am from the Carrier Sekani Tribal Council and I've come to learn about Shannen's Dream."

"*Kwe Kwe*, Spirit Bear!" said the children.

"Wow! You all speak Algonquin?" I was *beary* impressed!

"We are learning," one of my new friends, Chelsea, said. "The Elders are teaching us—and they're teaching us lots of other things too!"

Shannen's Dream

31

"My Uncle Huckleberry and friend Lak'insxw told me if I wanted to learn about First Nations schools, I had to ask children about Shannen's Dream. Can you teach me about it?"

The children nodded. We all sat in a circle so they could take turns telling me the story.

"After the Residential Schools closed," Chelsea said, "people in First Nations, Métis, and Inuit communities wanted their children to go to good schools, where they could be proud of their cultures and speak their languages."

"That sounds a lot better than Residential Schools!" I said. "Yes," Chelsea answered. "But because the government gives First Nations schools less money than other schools, it's a lot harder for Elders and teachers to help the students learn. Shannen didn't think this was fair—and neither do we."

REPORT CARD FOR CANADA

FAIRNESS FOR FIRST NATIONS
CHILDREN IN EDUCATION

Needs Improvement

"See those blue flowers, Spirit Bear?" asked a girl named Serena. "Those were Shannen Koostachin's favourite flowers. We planted them for her because she is our hero."

"They are beautiful," I said.

"Shannen was from the Attawapiskat First Nation in northern Ontario," Serena said. "When she looked up at the night sky and saw the Big Dipper, just like her ancestors had, it made her happy."

I thought about how the Big Dipper had shown me the way to the garden. "Wow! I like the Big Dipper, too. It guided me to all of you. The Big Dipper must be sacred to people *and* bears!"

"You are right Spirit Bear," Serena said. "It is. And Shannen loved it.

"Shannen loved learning too. She spoke two languages—Cree and English," said Serena. "But the only school in her community closed because tons of diesel fuel—that's like gasoline—leaked out of a pipe underneath the school. Over 30,000 gallons!"

I felt worried. "All of that fuel must have made the people and animals sick!"

"Yes, it did!" said Serena. "So the government brought up trailers for the children to learn in until a new school was built. They put the trailers on top of the old school's playground, and that is where Shannen went to school.

"The government promised the children a new school. But they didn't keep their promise and the trailers started falling apart."

A boy named Charlie piped up. "Spirit Bear, it got so bad that there was *ice* on the inside of the classrooms. Mice would sometimes eat kids' lunches! The teachers tried hard, but they didn't have many books or much gym or science equipment to teach the kids with.

"So Shannen and her friends in Attawapiskat decided to make a video showing other children, like us, how hard it was to learn there," said Charlie. "Shannen said things were so bad that kids were dropping out in Grade 4!"

I shook my head. School is supposed to be a good place. A safe place, for all children.

39

Chelsea spoke up again. "We saw the video and wanted to help. So when Shannen and her friends came to Ottawa in 2008 to ask the government to fix First Nations schools, we went to support them.

"Shannen knew that some First Nations communities have good schools, but many don't. It is hard for kids to learn and feel proud of who they are when their school is falling apart, or full of mould, or when they don't have proper books and other things to learn with."

"She wasn't just standing up for her school in Attawapiskat," Serena said. "She was asking for a proper school for every First Nations community that needed one.

"Shannen told the government, 'School is a time for dreams and every kid deserves this!' She asked us never to give up until every child had a proper school."

41

The children became quiet. They looked over at the flowers.

A boy named Daxton said quietly, "Then something sad happened, Spirit Bear. Shannen moved far away from her home in Attawapiskat to go to high school. One night, in 2010, she passed away in a car accident. She was only fifteen.

"We were sad," he went on. "But we also knew we had a promise to keep. We are going to make sure Shannen's Dream comes true!" The children all nodded.

I wiped away a tear. "Even though she was young, Shannen was a teacher. She reminds us to stand up for what is right."

"Yes!" Daxton said. "And that is why kids across Canada keep writing letters to the government, asking them to treat First Nations children fairly by making Shannen's Dream come true."

"Wow!" I said. "Do you think the letters are helping?"

"Yes!" my friends said happily.

"A new school in Attawapiskat opened in 2014," Chelsea said. "The words *Shannen's Dream* are written above the door. But we still write letters to the government because there are many more First Nations students who need good schools."

"We are going to write more letters to the government today, in all the languages we speak at home. We won't stop until *every* First Nations child has a good school!" said Daxton, taking my paw. "Do you want to join us, Spirit Bear?"

"I can *bearly* wait!" I said. "This is just what my mom teaches me. Everyone is sacred just the way they are and when we see someone who is not being treated right, we need to help make things better! I will write a letter in my language—Bear!"

We all cheered! We knew we could make a difference. I knew in my heart that if we all worked together, we could make Shannen's Dream come true for every First Nations student.

47

Dear Uncle Huckleberry,

Look up at the stars in the Big Dipper tonight. If you look closely, you'll see Shannen lighting the way. Shannen knew that school should be a time for dreams. My new friends and I will never give up until all First Nations students have safe and comfy schools!

Tell Lak'insxw that she was right. The ancestors did guide me to the children. Uncle Huckleberry... can you teach me to fish like they did when I come home again?

Love,
Spirit Bear

P.S. There's a special website about Shannen's Dream. You can visit it at shannensdream.ca

Shannen's Dream Timeline

1976 Attawapiskat gets its first elementary school, named J.R. Nakogee Elementary School.

1979 30,000 gallons of diesel fuel leak into the ground right under J.R. Nakogee school.

1980–2000 Children and teachers attending the school get sick from the fuel leak. The government sends people to look into the problem, but not much is done.

July 12, 1994 Shannen Koostachin is born to proud parents, Jenny Nakogee and Andrew Koostachin.

May 2000 The people of Attawapiskat close the elementary school because it is unsafe.

2000–2001 The government sets up portable trailers on top of the old school's playground and promises to build a new school.

2005 The government again promises the children of Attawapiskat a new school, but nothing is done. The portable trailers start breaking down. Black mould, mice, and ice inside classrooms are serious problems.

2006–2007 The government repeats its promise of a new school. Plans are made but nothing is done.

2007 Tired of broken promises for a new school and the horrible conditions in the portable trailers, Shannen (who is now in Grade 8) and her friends start the Attawapiskat School campaign.

May 2008 Shannen and two other students travel to Ottawa to meet with the government to ask for a new school. The government says they cannot afford it. Shannen tells them she "will never give up because school is a time for dreams and every kid deserves this."

June 1, 2010 Shannen Koostachin passes away in a car accident while attending high school hundreds of miles away from her home in Attawapiskat.

November 17, 2010 The children of Attawapiskat launch the Shannen's Dream campaign to continue Shannen's work to get proper schools and fair education funding for all First Nations students.

February 27, 2012 All Members of Parliament—the people elected to the House of Commons—vote to support Shannen's Dream (Private Members' Motion 201).

September 7, 2013 Famous First Nations (Abenaki) filmmaker Alanis Obomsawin's documentary about Shannen's Dream, called *Hi-Ho Mistahey!*, premieres at the Toronto International Film Festival.

August 27, 2014 A new elementary school opens in Attawapiskat. A sign is later placed above the door, reading "Shannen's Dream."

December 6, 2016 A report by the Office of the Parliamentary Budget Officer—a group that keeps watch on government spending—shows that First Nations students are only getting up to half the education funding of other students.

Today We are still working to make Shannen's Dream a reality. You can help! Find out more at shannensdream.ca.

Find learning resources and fun and free ways you can help at:
fncaringsociety.com